For my mother, thinking of our dolls' house – HW

For George and Ted – SL

STRIPES PUBLISHING LIMITED
An imprint of the Little Tiger Group
1 Coda Studios, 189 Munster Road,
London SW6 6AW

Imported into the EEA by Penguin Random House Ireland,
Morrison Chambers, 32 Nassau Street, Dublin D02 YH68

A paperback original
First published in Great Britain in 2021

Text copyright © Holly Webb, 2021
Illustrations copyright © Sarah Lodge, 2021
Author photograph copyright © Charlotte Knee Photography

ISBN: 978-1-78895-189-0

The Forest Stewardship Council® (FSC®) is a global, not-for-profit organization dedicated to the promotion of responsible forest management worldwide. FSC® defines standards based on agreed principles for responsible forest stewardship that are supported by environmental, social, and economic stakeholders. To learn more, visit www.fsc.org

10 9 8 7 6 5 4 3 2 1

Museum Kittens

The Sleepover Mystery

Holly Webb

Illustrated by Sarah Lodge

LITTLE TIGER

LONDON

Ground Floor

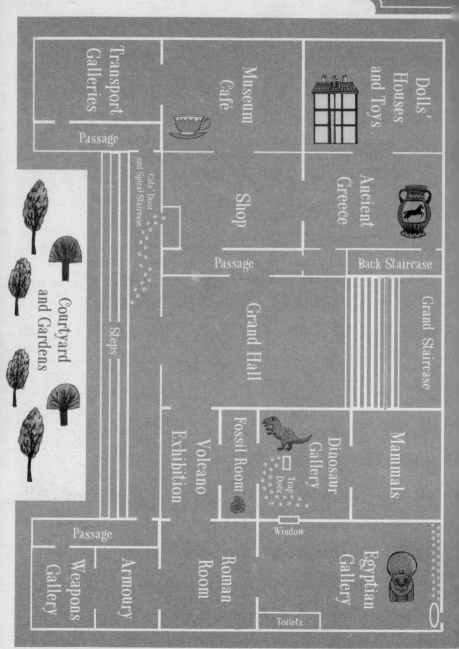

Transport Galleries

Passage

Museum Café

Shop

Dolls' Houses and Toys

Ancient Greece

Passage

Back Staircase

Cats' Door and Spiral Staircase

Courtyard and Gardens

Steps

Grand Hall

Grand Staircase

Volcano Exhibition

Fossil Room

Dinosaur Gallery

Mammals

Trap Door

Window

Passage

Armoury

Roman Room

Egyptian Gallery

Weapons Gallery

Toilets

Map

First Floor

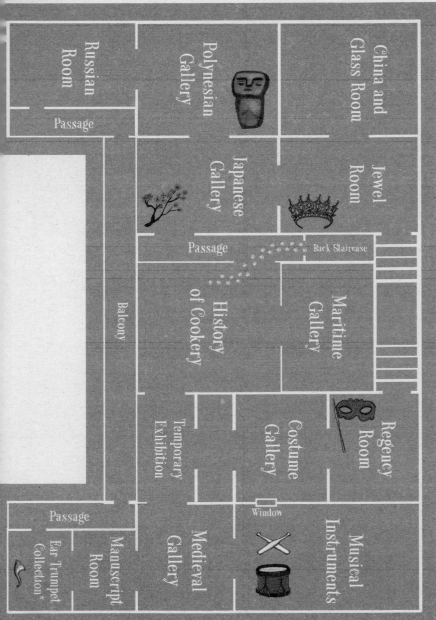

Russian Room

Passage

Polynesian Gallery

China and Glass Room

Jewel Room

Japanese Gallery

Passage

Back Staircase

Balcony

History of Cookery

Maritime Gallery

Temporary Exhibition

Costume Gallery

Regency Room

Window

Passage

Ear Trumpet Collection*

Manuscript Room

Medieval Gallery

Musical Instruments

Mrs Jane Martlesham Bequest

❧ Chapter One ❧

The kittens were lazing away the
afternoon around the courtyard fountain,
resting before their night shift. Ever since
they'd managed to save the precious
Egyptian Gallery from a flood a few
weeks earlier, they'd been given their own
guard shifts at the museum. All four of
the kittens were very proud of their new
duties. They loved prowling around the

galleries, sniffing for rats and mice, and maybe even burglars.

But although they didn't work as many hours as the older cats yet, they were all getting short on sleep. It was making Boris grumpy. The ginger kitten and his fluffy white sister Bianca seemed to spend most of the time snapping at each other. Tasha, their tabby sister, was worried that the pair were going to get them all into trouble with their constant squabbling. She had to keep reminding Bianca and Boris that they were supposed to be quiet and well behaved when the museum was open…

Peter, the black kitten, was just keeping out of it. He hadn't been living at the museum for very long, so he tried not to get in the way when Boris and

Bianca fought. He knew he was a proper museum cat now, but that didn't mean he was actually one of the family.

Boris and Bianca were being even snappier than usual this week. The Egyptian Gallery was open again, but the flood had caused a lot of damage and it had been really expensive to tidy everything up. So the Museum Director had thought of a brilliant way to bring in lots of visitors. At the end of the week, the museum was having its first school sleepover. Sixty children were going to stay overnight in the Dinosaur Gallery! The whole museum was full of staff having the jitters and arguing over the tiniest things, and now Boris and Bianca were joining in too.

"It's your turn!" Bianca hissed.

"No, it isn't." Boris curled his tail round his hind paws. "Definitely not."

"I did it last week!"

"Mmmm, well, I can't remember when I last did it, but it's absolutely not my turn." Boris yawned.

"Oh!" Bianca mewed in frustration. "You're so lazy! Just because you don't like the China and Glass Room. Because it doesn't have boring old suits of armour, or motor cars like in the Transport Galleries. You can't pick and choose, you know."

"That's nonsense." Boris shook his whiskers and yawned again, then collapsed down into a patch of sunlight. "I guard all the different galleries when it's my turn. And right now it isn't." He opened one eye to peer at Bianca. "Are you saying Ma's got the shift rota wrong?"

"I'll do it," Tasha put in. Her tabby ears were flickering back and forth as she listened to her brother and sister sniping at each other. She hated it when the other kittens argued.

"Excellent," Boris purred. "I'll take the Dinosaur Gallery then."

"No!" Bianca glared at Tasha. "Don't you dare!"

"But I thought you wanted someone to guard the China and Glass— " Tasha started to say.

"I want *him* to do it, because it's *his* turn! Ma hasn't got the rota wrong, he's just not listening because he doesn't want to do as he's told!" Bianca was practically spitting with fury now, and Tasha could tell that Boris was deliberately provoking her. He had his eyes almost closed as if he was asleep, but she could see a bright amber flash every so often as he sneaked glances at Bianca.

"But does it really matter, so long as

someone does it…" she tried to say to
Bianca.

"Yes, it does. It isn't fair!" Bianca
snarled. "Oh, how can you be so stupid!"

"Hey! Don't call her that." Peter sat up,
his whiskers bristling.

"But she's doing exactly what Boris
wants!" Bianca wailed. "Look! Look at
him – he thinks it's funny!"

Tasha and Peter looked obediently.
Boris *was* shaking with purry laughter.

"You still shouldn't say Tasha's stupid."
Peter came to stand beside the tabby
kitten. "She was only trying to help."

"And I like the China and Glass Room,"
Tasha said. "I don't mind guarding it."

Boris opened his eyes. "No one likes
the China and Glass. It's the boringest

room in the whole museum. Except for the one with those ear trumpets."

"The what?" Peter blinked. How could anyone play a trumpet with their ears?

"Ear trumpets," Tasha explained. "An old lady left loads of money to the museum in her will a few years ago, but she said they could only have the money if they found a room to put her collection of ear trumpets in. It's along the balcony, next to the Manuscript Room."

"Oh … *those* things. I wondered what they were." Peter nodded politely. "Do they sound nice?"

Boris yawned. "No idea. No one ever plays them."

Tasha wrinkled her muzzle. "Boris! You *know* they aren't *that* sort of trumpet. They're for helping people who can't hear very well," she explained to Peter. "You put one end in your ear and people shout into the other end. But I'm not sure they ever actually worked. No one uses them now."

"Mmmnnnn…" Boris let out another yawn. "I just guard the museum, Tasha, I don't read all the labels."

Even Tasha was giving her brother an irritable stare now and Bianca was looking smug.

"Anyway," Boris went on. "The China and Glass Room is very, very boring. Pots. And vases. And teensy little wine glasses.

Who wants to look at those when they could have a big, shiny suit of armour? That school sleepover that's happening in a couple of days – the children aren't sleeping in the super-exciting China and Glass Room, are they?"

"It *is* exciting!" Tasha put in. "China is made of bones."

"Bones? No, it isn't," Boris said. He'd clearly decided that today was his day to be as annoying as possible.

"It is! Bones and clay and some other things. Ground up very fine."

"Is it really?" Peter asked, feeling slightly more interested in the china now.

"Yes, but only the kind that says bone china on the label," Tasha admitted.

"Goodness." Peter shuddered. "I never knew *that*."

"And glass is made out of sand," Tasha went on.

The other three kittens stared at her.

"It can't be," Bianca said. "It would fall apart. Anyway, that's not the point. Whatever the stuff's made out of, it's Boris's turn to be on watch in there and he has to do it."

"Nope."

"Yes, you will!" Bianca screeched, losing her temper. "You will, you will, you will!"

"Can't make me." Boris yawned again, sneaking a sideways look at his sister.

The thick white fur stood up all the way along Bianca's spine and her tail fluffed out like a feather duster. She arched her back and jumped up and down on all four paws, like one of the strange springy jack-in-the-boxes in the Dolls' Houses and Toys Gallery. Tasha edged away, convinced for a moment that there were sparks flying off her sister's fur.

Bianca yowled and leaped on Boris.

Boris was so surprised that for a few seconds he sat there like a lump – with Bianca clinging on to his back. Then he hissed and stood up, shaking himself wildly from side to side to fling Bianca off. The white kitten went flying and Boris spun round, glaring at her.

Unfortunately, he forgot that he was

delicately balanced on the edge of a
fountain. His claws scrabbled and slid
– and he splashed into the basin with a
shriek of fury.

Bianca peered down at him, looking
shocked, and then her whiskers twitched
with delight. She hadn't actually meant to
push Boris into the pool, but he deserved
it!

"Good!" she sniggered. "You were
looking very grubby."

"Rrrrr!" Boris growled loudly as he surged out of the water, wearing a panicked goldfish on his head. He was usually a very easy-going cat, but just occasionally he lost his temper. There was a wild look in his eyes now and Bianca edged back round the side of the fountain. Boris snaked after her, shaking his ears and dripping everywhere. "Look!" he snarled. "I'm all wet!"

"It's a nice day, you'll soon dry," Peter said soothingly. He and Tasha exchanged worried glances. This was turning into a proper catfight!

Boris crept along the rim of the fountain, ears low and tail lashing, and Bianca let out a squeak. She turned and leaped down from the fountain, streaking across the courtyard with Boris close behind. Tasha and Peter raced after them.

Tasha gasped as she saw her sister shoot into the main hall and up the marble staircase. "Bianca, no!" she mewed. "It's not closing time yet!"

As the museum cats weren't really meant to be in the galleries during the day, they relied on a complicated system of tunnels and pipes and passages to get around. But with Boris looking at her like that, Bianca decided she didn't care. She dashed through the Regency Room and into the Costume Gallery, with Boris hissing like a kettle just behind her.

Bianca adored the Costume Gallery – it was her second favourite room, after the Jewels – and she knew it far better than

Boris did. She was hoping to be able to dart into a shadowy corner and hide until he had calmed down.

But Boris was still too close. Bianca had no chance to disappear into any of her usual hidey-holes. She risked a look over her shoulder – perhaps Boris wasn't quite so furious now?

Bianca shivered. She was quite sure she could see every single one of his teeth. Desperate now, she did what all panicked cats do – she went high. She clawed her way up one of the

costume exhibits, a beautiful
stiff silk Venetian ballgown
with pearl embroidery.

A stiff silk Venetian
ballgown with pearl
embroidery and long, dark
tears all down the skirt.

The fragile fabric
ripped
to shreds
as soon as
it met Bianca's
claws.

Chapter Two

"Look what you did!" Boris said, his eyes wide. The damage to a museum exhibit was enough to jolt him out of his fury and he stopped short, skidding the last half metre and almost crashing into the ballgown.

"Ohhh…" Bianca hung there with her claws sunk into the gathers at the waistline, her eyes closed. "Ohhh…
Is it ripped?"

"Um … yes," Peter murmured. He and Tasha had appeared beside Boris, panting. They had gone as fast as they could, but they'd been trying to keep out of sight.

"What were you thinking?" Tasha hissed at them both. "People saw you!"

Peter nudged her hard with his shoulder, nodding towards the ballgown, where Bianca dangled like an odd little furry purse.

"Get down from there," Tasha said urgently. "Visitors are going to come in here any minute. Maybe even one of the staff!"

"I can't! I can't!" Bianca wailed. "My claws are stuck and I don't want to open my eyes. This dress is so beautiful and it's

all covered in pearls – it's my favourite
and I tooooore it!"

"We can't climb up there and get you,"
Peter called to her. "We'll
make it worse."

Bianca whined sadly
and tried to unhook one
set of claws. The gathered
waist gave a little as a
few stitches broke, and
she slid down the silk
in a flurry of white fur.
She landed at the feet of
the other three kittens and
closed her eyes again firmly.

"How bad is it?" she asked.

Tasha exchanged glances with Boris
and Peter. "I expect they can mend it,"

she murmured. "They're very good at mending things, the museum people. Hopefully they'll think it was the rats. Or – or age…" She wasn't sure if that was true, but Bianca was so upset, Tasha wanted to cheer her up.

Bianca opened one eye a slit and glanced up at the ballgown. Then she shuddered and turned away. "Look what I did…" she whispered. Her whiskers crackled straight again and she opened her eyes wide, glaring at Boris. "This is all your fault!"

Boris gaped at her. "What? It wasn't me that sunk my claws into a priceless exhibit!"

"And I wouldn't have either, if you hadn't been chasing me!"

"You pushed me into a fountain! Oh, I'm not listening to this," Boris muttered. He stomped away through the Costume Gallery, his ears flat and furious.

"I wonder if they've noticed yet," Bianca whispered. She was sitting in their nest of old tapestries in the cats' cellar home. For once, Tasha was grooming her sister, instead of the other way round. It was the only thing she could think of to make Bianca feel better. But Bianca was fretful and wriggly.

"Oh, stop it, you're smoothing my fur the wrong way," she snapped, twisting away. "Leave me alone."

Tasha backed off with a sigh and curled

up next to Peter, watching her sister and brother anxiously. Bianca and Boris had been arguing ever since they'd all sneaked out of the Costume Gallery. Now it was hours later, nearly time for the evening shifts to start, and still no one had agreed on whose turn it was to guard China and Glass.

"Kittens! Did you have anything to do with the furore upstairs in the Costume Gallery?" Tasha's mother, Smoke, stalked into the cellar and eyed the kittens suspiciously. "I've just seen one of the conservationists up there in tears. The poor woman couldn't even speak! The other staff had to take her away and feed her chocolate biscuits and tea in the café. And they've removed a dress from the display! They seem to think it was a rat, but those rips looked remarkably like kitten clawmarks to me..." She peered more closely at Boris. "What on earth have you done to your fur? It's all spiky and strange."

Tasha and Peter exchanged guilty looks, and Boris and Bianca immediately started trying to blame each other.

"It was her!"

"It was him!"

Smoke sat down heavily next to them and narrowed her eyes. "What did you do?" she sighed.

"He was chasing me," Bianca said hurriedly. "And I was so scared that I didn't think and I ran up the dress."

"Bianca!" Smoke swished her fluffy dark grey tail. "I'm surprised at you."

Bianca hung her head. "I never meant to," she muttered. "It was all his fault…"

"Did you chase her?" Smoke asked Boris.

"Yes," Boris admitted. "But only because she jumped on my back and sank her claws in. I fell in the fountain!"

"He's so lazy!" Bianca burst out. "He won't take his proper turn at guarding."

"And it's up to you to make sure Boris

works hard enough?" Smoke asked, eyeing Bianca with her head on one side.

"Well, no, but…"

"I had thought my kittens were becoming real museum cats, but obviously not." Smoke fixed Peter with a glare. "And they're clearly having a very bad influence on you."

"Oh … er…" Peter stammered, not quite sure what to say. At least she hadn't put it the other way round. But he did think Smoke was being a little unfair on him and Tasha.

"You can all stay down here and sleep tonight – there'll be no shifts for any of you."

The kittens gazed at each other in dismay as Smoke stalked away. "Did …

did she mean *never*?" Peter said, his eyes round with horror.

Tasha gave a tiny mew. "I was supposed to be guarding the toys tonight," she whispered. "I love the toys…"

"Thanks," Boris said bitterly to Bianca, and she hissed.

"Please don't start quarrelling all over again!" Tasha pleaded, trying to nudge noses with Bianca. But her sister stood up and marched away from the soft heap of tapestries, curling up on her own on a torn and holey curtain in the corner of the cellar.

Boris turned his back on them and appeared to go to sleep, but Tasha wasn't sure if he was pretending. She certainly couldn't sleep. She could feel Bianca's aloneness, cold and miserable in the corner.

Quietly, she crept out of the huddle of black and ginger fur that was Peter and Boris, and padded across the dusty stone floor to her sister.

"What do you want?" Bianca muttered as Tasha snuggled on to the old curtain beside her.

"Just to make sure you're all right. I didn't want you to feel guilty."

"I don't feel guilty," Bianca growled. "It was all Boris's fault for chasing me and he knows it. I'd only be feeling guilty if I'd done something wrong. And I didn't. Now leave me alone!"

Several floors above, in the Dolls' Houses and Toys Gallery, there was a scritchy tapping of little feet.

"I tell you, there's food here," one excited rat hissed to the others. "Cakes. Puddings. Pies. A whole fish, although I have to admit it's quite a small one."

"I'm not sure about this, Luther," said Morris, peering up at the dolls' house – a particularly smart one, with a blue-painted roof and a balcony. "Wouldn't someone have noticed already if there were so many tasty treats? It doesn't smell like food. Everything smells old, like it's been here for years."

"Real cakes?" asked Pip, the smallest

rat, ignoring Morris entirely. "With cream and sugar and little icing roses?"

All three rats turned to stare at him and Pip's whiskers drooped. "I just like eating things that are pretty," he said wistfully. "Leftovers and scraps always look a bit grey. Now they've got those kittens guarding too, we hardly ever get to swipe the good stuff from the café."

"I don't think they can be cream cakes," Dusty told him kindly. "Cream would go off, and Morris is right – everything in here is old."

"Stop waffling," Luther snapped.

"Ooooh … waffles…" Pip sighed, and then he pretended that he hadn't said anything when Luther glared at him.

"Come on. Up we go. Keep an eye

out for those dratted cats, they're everywhere."

All four rats scrambled up the wooden plinth and peered curiously in at the windows of the huge old dolls' house.

"I told you! There's a whole kitchen in there," Luther said, hanging upside down off the balcony. "Look at all that food on the table."

"Look at that cake..." Pip pressed his nose up against the thin glass of the windows. How do we get in?"

"There's a door," Dusty pointed out, trying not to roll her eyes. "But I don't think—"

Luther and Pip had already barged the front door open, and were barrelling eagerly into the kitchen. It was full of tiny furniture, and a wooden dresser wobbled as the rats bounced about. A miniature copper jelly mould teetered and fell, landing hard on Luther's head. The big rat pushed it up out of his eyes and looked eagerly at the laden table. So many deliciousnesses…

Pip seized a tall pink and white layer cake in his paws, closing his eyes as he bit into a sugar rose. "Ugh! Ow! My teeth…" He spat out little pink pieces and glared at the cake.

"Is it off?" Morris asked sympathetically, peering round the door. "Bit stale?"

"It's made of plaster…" Pip said dolefully. "All of it. Even the fish."

🐾 Chapter Three 🐾

The next morning, Bianca had disappeared from the cellars before the other kittens woke up.

Tasha peered around, confused, and then nudged Peter. "Where is she?" she muttered. "Did you see her go?"

Peter only blinked and purred, and Tasha sighed. He was no help.

They did see Bianca for a few minutes

when the Old Man, the caretaker whose job it was to look after the cats, dished up their breakfast. But she burrowed in among a clutch of uncles and aunts, and pretended not to notice that Tasha was staring at her. After breakfast she slipped away again, without a word to the other kittens.

"She's sulking," Boris pointed out. "Two can play at that game. Or four, I mean."

"I don't want to sulk," Tasha mewed. "I want her to be happy. I know Bianca's mean sometimes, but I hate it when she's not talking to us. Everything feels wrong."

Boris sniffed, but then he licked his paw and gave one ear a thoughtful wash. Maybe there was something in what Tasha was saying. It felt strange to be only three kittens again. As though there was a corner missing.

"We could go and look for her," he said slowly. "Not to say sorry! Just … we could see if she wants to go and look at the Jewel Room. And maybe I'll take the first shift in China and Glass, when we're allowed to start guarding again."

Smoke had decided the kittens needed a rest from their guard duty – that they were too tired and it was making them grumpy and silly. Peter, Tasha and Boris had to admit that maybe she was right, but they were desperate to prove they could be proper museum cats again.

"You're a very good brother," Tasha said, rubbing her chin lovingly against his, and Boris looked grand and noble.

"Let's go and find her!"

But when they finally came across Bianca in the courtyard garden, sunning herself on the stone plinth of one of the statues, all she did was yawn at them.

"I'm too sleepy to look at jewels," she said haughtily. "Would you mind moving? You're in my sun."

Even Tasha felt quite cross with her after that, and Peter and Boris were all for pushing her in the fountain this time.

All day they caught glimpses of Bianca in the gardens, being admired by visitors. She must have had her photo taken a hundred times, making huge eyes and purring for the camera.

"Look at her, she's at it again," Boris said, his whiskers bristling as they spotted Bianca surrounded by a crowd of schoolchildren.

"She does love being fussed over," Tasha sighed, watching one of the girls pick Bianca up and snuggle the white kitten under her chin. "I suppose it's much more fun than being with us."

"Pffft. She'll stop it soon. Bianca's a museum cat," Peter said. He seemed to think being a museum cat was more important than the others did. Tasha had decided it was probably because he hadn't been born in the museum. Perhaps she and Boris and Bianca took it all for granted. To Peter, the museum was always special.

"But she shouldn't be hanging around them like that," he said now, watching disapprovingly as Bianca trotted after the schoolchildren into the Grand Hall. "We aren't allowed in there! After what happened yesterday too… We've got to be perfect – at least until your mother lets us start taking shifts again."

"Bianca's still upset about that dress," Tasha said worriedly. "That's why she's being so silly." What she didn't say out loud was, *She just wants everyone to love her*. Tasha felt a tiny shiver run through her whiskers. Bianca was almost like a pet today, trotting after those children. She didn't look like a museum cat at all.

The party of schoolchildren were being
shown around the galleries during the
day and then they were going to watch a
film. They had all brought sleeping bags so
they could camp out under the dinosaur
skeletons. Some of the cats still weren't
very sure about this.

Neither was the Old Man, who was used
to being the only human wandering about
the museum at night. He disapproved
entirely and he had been muttering about
it for days. "Lot of nonsense. Sleeping
under a skeleton. Catch their death, I
shouldn't wonder."

Seeing the children bouncing excitedly
all over the museum, Tasha, Peter and

Boris were more worried about the exhibits. Sixty children seemed very *loud*. Usually they could breathe a sigh of relief at closing time, when even the noisiest visitors went home. It seemed very odd that these ones were staying.

"Look at Bianca," Boris hissed disgustedly. "She's got that little girl with the plaits carrying her around now! What does she think she is, one of those cuddly toys they sell in the gift shop?"

The museum sold quite a few different animals, and Tasha had seen Bianca admiring their sparkling eyes and silky fur. Bianca would love to be a toy, she thought, being cuddled and having her fur brushed all the time.

"She's a disgrace," Boris muttered.

"Sooner or later one of those teachers is going to notice her," Peter said. "At the moment they're more worried about that pair over there who keep trying to climb up the stegosaurus, but Bianca needs to watch out. We ought to warn her."

Tasha nodded and Boris heaved a huge sigh. "We don't want Ma finding out we've got into any more trouble, I suppose," he said. "That teacher just said they were going to the Egyptian Gallery to see the mummies. We can nip down to the cellars and come up through the passage, so no one sees us."

The three of them hurried back to their cellar home and then scurried through one of the dark tunnels that honeycombed the museum. They arrived in the Egyptian

Gallery a few minutes later and peered round the huge mummy case.

"Ugh," Tasha said. "That tunnel smells odd. I'm not sure it dried out properly after the flood. Do you feel damp, or is just me?"

"I think it's only because we're remembering the water," Peter murmured, shuddering a little. "Look, there she is!"

Bianca was twining herself round the ankles of the girl with the plaits.

"Pssst!" Tasha hissed at her. "Pssst, Bianca!"

Bianca looked at them round the girl's white socks. "What?" she whispered. "I'm busy with Anya."

Anya? The three kittens exchanged a look.

"Watch out, they've got teachers with them," Tasha warned. "You'll be in trouble if you're seen."

Bianca's blue eyes flashed and she stalked over to Anya's other side, very deliberately ignoring her sister.

"Oi, Bianca!" Boris growled. "We're already in disgrace with Ma! Come away from them!"

Bianca shot back round, glaring. "You're just jealous! They think I'm sweet, they said so! Nobody thinks you're sweet, Boris. You're lazy. You're a slob! All three of you are jealous because people love me. I don't need to hang around with silly little kittens!"

Peter, Tasha and Boris stared open-mouthed as the crowd of children wandered away to look at the statues in the Roman Room, and Bianca trotted off after them.

"Did you see that?" Dusty said, her whiskers twitching with nosiness.

The rats had been following the children all morning and they thoroughly approved of this sleepover business. The children had food. They could smell it – sweets in pockets, packets of crisps in backpacks. And they were staying all night! There would be plenty of opportunities for pilfering. They needed something to cheer themselves up. Not only had the dolls' house food turned out to be entirely made of plaster, but the paint had tasted disgusting when they'd licked it. And Pip's teeth still hurt.

"What?" Luther didn't even glance round.

"That little white cat. She's not talking to the others."

"So?" Luther growled, but Morris's tail curled.

"You mean…"

"She's alone, yes," Dusty said thoughtfully. "Well, she's with those grubby children *now*, but they'll have to leave soon. And then we'll have a little white kitten all on her own…" She rubbed her paws together and gave a ratty chuckle. "I'm seeing a chance for us to get our own back on those nasty, busybody cats. Why don't we put them in a proper spot of bother?"

❧ Chapter Four ❧

Bianca crept through the museum,
her paws silent as silk. She'd had to make
an appearance at supper, even though
she wasn't all that hungry. She didn't
want Ma fussing around trying to find
her or, worse still, Grandpa Ivan. He'd
already noticed that she wasn't talking to
the others. He'd cornered her at supper
and given her one of his sharp looks.

Bianca wasn't sure how he managed to
see so much, when he only had one eye.

"All on your own, little
miss?" he'd growled.

Bianca had opened
her eyes very wide and
tried to look innocent,
but the old white cat
hadn't been having any
of it.

"Whatever squabble
you've had with the others,
you'd be better off swallowing your pride.
You'll regret it if you don't, white-kitten-
whose-name-I'll-remember-in-a-minute."

Silly old Grandpa, Bianca thought
crossly as she made her way to the
Dinosaur Gallery. What did he know

about it? Why should she have to hang around in the cellars with the other kittens when there were people who actually wanted to see her? She had been stroked and petted and called beautiful all day, and she had loved it. If she stayed down in the cellars, she would be sleeping on her own, curled up on a musty old curtain. Up in the gallery, there were soft, cosy sleeping bags to lie on. With nice warm children inside.

She padded into the room, which was dimly greenish in the emergency lighting, and looked around for Anya, the girl with the blond plaits. Some of the children were still awake, she noticed, although they were pretending that they weren't. There were a few bars of chocolate being carefully shared around.

"Kitten," someone whispered. "Here, kitten, here, puss…"

Anya was right there, Bianca realized, almost next to the door. Purring a little, she went to sniff at her sleeping bag.

"I hoped you'd come," Anya murmured, sitting up to stroke her. "I don't like it in here in the dark." She shivered a little. "It was fun in the daytime, but now all those skeletons look like they're grinning at us. And there are the mummies – Lucy and Jack said the mummies might wake up in the middle of the night and walk around! They said they were going to see if they could wake one up, once we've all gone to sleep…"

Bianca heard Anya's breath catch and she peered up at her worriedly. Gently, she nudged the top of her head against the girl's hand.

"Oh! You're such a nice cat. I'm glad you're here. I keep hearing weird noises. Like little scuttly footsteps."

Anya rubbed Bianca behind her ears and the kitten nuzzled her fingers. Scuttly footsteps? Bianca sniffed thoughtfully. Were there rats about? Probably they could smell those sweets just like she could.

I'm not going to let any rats frighten the children, Bianca thought to herself, peering around fiercely. Her tail fluffed up a little and she flattened her ears. Then she climbed on top of the sleeping bag and stomped up and down on Anya's feet, padding furiously at the soft material and making Anya giggle.

"You're so funny," the girl said, sounding happier.

Bianca purred. Sometimes, just sometimes, she wondered if it might be nice to be a different sort of cat. The sort of cat who slept on a child's bed every night, rather than sitting up in the dark keeping watch for rats.

Why should she have to work so hard, when no one cared about her? Ma had been so cross about that torn dress and Bianca was sure none of it was *her* fault. Sometimes she wasn't sure she fitted in the same way the others did. Peter seemed to belong perfectly, and he hadn't even been born at the museum!

Perhaps she just wasn't meant to be a museum kitten.

It was a very odd thought, rather frightening. Bianca felt as if the bottom had dropped out of her stomach. She didn't really mean that, did she? Then Anya gave a gasp of horror and Bianca's head shot up.

"That noise! It's those horrible little scrabbly footsteps again..." Anya whispered.

Silhouetted against the brighter light from the doorway was a dark, threatening shape. The humpbacked shape of a rat, teeth bared, crouched to spring.

The rat hissed and time slowed for Bianca.

She heard Anya whimper in fright and a surge of fury ran through her. There were other children awake too – she could hear worried whispering and one of them was starting to cry. For someone who a moment before had wondered if she was meant to be a museum kitten, Bianca was on guard at once. Her fur rose up and she hissed back, showing as many teeth as she could. No child was going to be terrified by a rat while she was in the museum!

The rat darted away and Bianca flew after it, bounding

through the gallery. She was so furious that she hadn't thought about what would happen if she *caught* the rat. She only knew that she had to protect the children.

Strangely, the rat didn't bolt down any of its holes, the way the rats usually did. Instead, it kept on dashing in and out of different galleries, with Bianca always trailing a little way behind. It was very fast, Bianca thought, feeling the ache in her front paws. Really very, very fast.

She was trying so hard to keep up that she hardly noticed the way the rat seemed to change colour. It had been quite a dark brown when she first saw it in the Dinosaur Gallery, but in the volcano exhibit it was distinctly yellowish and while they were racing through Ancient

Greece it was quite grey…

Bianca put it down to the strange green emergency lighting.

She was gasping for breath by the time she chased the rat into the Dolls' Houses and Toys Gallery, and there was a horrible burning feeling in her chest. The gallery looked quite spooky in the night lighting, and Bianca shivered. The huge, spotted rocking horse was creaking to and fro, just a little…

The rat – which was pale grey now – dashed three times round

one of the dolls' houses. Then it was
cheeky enough to leap inside the open
front of the house and dance up and
down on the prettily set tea table in
the drawing
room.

Seething with fury, Bianca sprang after it. But it was only as she chased the rat's thick pink tail up the stairs that she remembered this dolls' house wasn't usually displayed with the front open. The visitors loved peering through the windows...

So why was it open now?

Bianca dashed after the rat into the nursery bedroom and then watched as it made a flying leap out of the front of the house. She was about to follow it when a strange shadow fell across the dolls' house. The hinged front of the house was closing, she realized. Bianca scrabbled her paws against the little tapestry rug, ready to fling herself after the rat – but the rug slipped from under her paws and tangled her up. Bianca skidded right into a window, mashing her nose up against the glass. Just below, she could see the rats, three of them, looking up at her and sniggering.

Then there was a delicate little click somewhere round the side of the house. Someone had just latched the dolls' house shut.

Chapter Five

Peter, Tasha and Boris hadn't tried to talk to Bianca at supper time. She'd obviously been trying to avoid them and they hadn't known what to say. But by the time the older cats had set off for their night shifts, Tasha was starting to feel anxious. She hadn't expected Bianca to come and apologize, but she had at least expected her to come back...

"Do you think we ought to say something?" Tasha whispered as the three kittens perched on the nest of worn tapestries.

"Who to?" Boris said. He tried to shrug, but it wasn't very convincing. Tasha was sure he was worried as well.

"Ma? Or Grandpa Ivan?" Tasha stood up, pacing round the other two. "She always comes back down to the cellars to sleep, everyone does unless they're on a guard shift. It feels all wrong without her here."

"If we go and tell Ma that Bianca's disappeared, she will be furious with her *and* with us. And then Bianca will say we're sneaks – she'll never speak to us again!" Boris pointed out. "She already hates me. We're not telling anyone anything."

Peter nudged him. "Boris…"

"No! We're not telling Ma!"

"Boris…" Tasha said nervously.

"I said no!"

"What aren't you telling me, Boris?" Smoke said from behind him, leaning over so that her long black whiskers tickled his nose.

Boris sat like a statue, thinking as fast as he could.

"Peter? Tasha? Seeing as the rat seems to have got your brother's tongue… Is he still arguing with Bianca, is that what this is about? Where *is* Bianca?"

Peter and Tasha stared at each other, wide-eyed. What should they say?

"We're … um … not sure where Bianca is," Tasha admitted. "She's not really talking to any of us. We're a bit worried about her."

Smoke sighed. "I think Bianca's more upset about that dress than any of us realized. I expect she's upstairs somewhere, thinking things through. I suggest you three get some sleep. She'll probably sneak back down here in the middle of the night, feeling sorry for herself." Smoke eyed Boris sternly. "And when she does, you won't be saying anything unkind, will you?"

"Me?" Boris muttered as Smoke stalked away to talk to one of the adult cats. "I'm not the one who says mean things. I can hardly ever *think* of anything mean to say. It's Bianca who's sharp-tongued. Honestly, this is so unfair. But I won't say anything to her," he added hurriedly as Tasha turned huge worried green eyes on him.

"I was hoping Ma would go and look for Bianca."

"Why? Ma's right. Bianca's upstairs in a sulk – she doesn't need us fussing," Boris said with a yawn. "Go to sleep, Tasha."

While Boris, Tasha and Peter were talking about her down in the cellars, Bianca was

trapped inside the beautiful old dolls'
house. She had been furious when the
front of the house first slammed shut.
Particularly because she'd hit her nose
quite hard on the nursery window and
she suspected that her whiskers were
creased. It was all very annoying, but
she hadn't panicked. She would escape
through a window, she thought. And
then she would chase after those cheeky
rats and teach them a lesson. How dare
they shut up a museum cat in one of the
exhibits! It was … it was…

It was embarrassing, Bianca admitted
to herself. She absolutely must not let the
other kittens know what had happened,
not ever. She could just imagine Boris
chortling away. *Oh, Bianca, that's what*

happens when you spend so much time fussing over your fur. People start to think you're a toy. Even Tasha and Peter would laugh. She needed to get out of here as quickly as possible. Besides, she had to go and make sure the children were all right. Those rats had really frightened Anya and the others. Bianca wasn't having that, not in her museum.

It was odd, she thought to herself, but Anya's scared face had made her feel quite differently about being a museum cat. She really had been wondering about leaving the museum and becoming a pet. But when she had seen a rat menacing the children, the surge of fury she felt had surprised her.

Bianca peered out of the nursery

window, trying to see if the rats were still there. They seemed to have disappeared. She sighed and shook out her crumpled whiskers. She had been planning to climb through the window but she couldn't. The glass was quite solid, too thick for her to break – not that she wanted to go around breaking anything. She was already in disgrace about the ballgown.

Did all the windows have glass in them? She squeezed herself through the nursery door on to the tiny landing and then into the master bedroom, which had a grand miniature four-poster bed. The windows in there had the same thick glass. Bianca's heart began to thud a little faster as she hurried down the steep wooden staircase to inspect the front door.

It was closed, but surely it was too small to have a lock? She just needed to push it open. She put out a paw and poked at the door. It rattled a bit but it didn't move. Bianca caught her breath sharply and then rolled her eyes. Of course. It was a door that needed to be pulled. She hooked her claws in between the door and the frame and tried to open it inwards – but still it didn't budge.

Bianca crouched down to peer at the tiny crack between the door and the wall. There was a catch – she remembered it now, a sort of hook to hold the front door closed. Her stomach seemed to turn over like the goldfish in the courtyard fountain. She felt all cold and squirmy.

The rats had trapped her.

There was no way to get out.

Tasha couldn't sleep. She twitched and wriggled and flicked her tail until Peter and Boris gave up trying too.

"Would you leave off!" Boris groaned at last. "I'm tired!"

"Shall we go and look for Bianca?" Peter sighed.

"Yes! Yes please!" Tasha jumped up and swiped her tongue lovingly over his ears. "I know you think I'm being silly, but I'm really worried about her. She never, *ever* sleeps away from us."

"She's probably in the Costume Gallery," Peter told her. "It's still one of her favourite places. Or she's fast asleep in the Jewel Room by the case with her favourite tiara."

"Well, if she is, we can come straight back here and go to sleep ourselves. And I'll give you both half my breakfast tomorrow."

Boris jumped up quickly when she said that. "Hurry up then! We'll try the dresses first." He led the way up the dusty passage from the cellars to the Egyptian Gallery, and then they darted out into the Grand Hall and up the staircase.

The Costume Gallery was dark and still as the three kittens peered round the doorway. The faint emergency lights made the room look like some strange silent party, full of figures in grand clothes. But there was no white kitten curled up on the hem of any of the dresses. Tasha went to look at the torn ballgown, but it was gone, replaced by a neat little printed notice – REMOVED FOR RENOVATION.

Boris ducked his head in embarrassment. "Maybe she wouldn't want to come up here," he said, his voice a low rumble.

"Let's try the jewels," Peter put in, and they padded away to the Jewel Room.

Bianca's bound to be here, Tasha thought hopefully. *The jewels would definitely cheer her up.* Bianca's favourite exhibit was a huge, diamond tiara made to look like a garland of flowers, with tiny sprays of emerald leaves curling round. Tasha could see the watery gleam of the diamond flowers from inside the glass case. She had hoped to see a small white cat curled up on top of the glass – Bianca liked to snooze next to her favourite jewels. But this room was empty too.

"Maybe the Egyptian Gallery – we didn't really look, we just ran straight through," Peter suggested. "She does like those golden scarab brooches. And there's gold on some of the coffins too. You know what she's like about sparkly things."

"Maybe," Tasha agreed doubtfully, and they hurried back down the marble staircase.

The Egyptian Gallery always put the kittens' fur on end when they peeped into it in the dark. It was packed with coffins and mummies and grave goods, for a start. There were even two small, sad mummified cats. But the worst thing was, since the flood, all of them seemed to hear the faint slosh and drip of water whenever they went inside.

"She's not here," Boris muttered. "Bianca's got more sense than that. I don't like it. I can smell the water, and I know there isn't any here."

"Me too," Tasha said, glad she wasn't the only one.

Peter shivered, and then his ears pricked forwards and the fur rose up all along his back as he heard soft, shuffling footsteps behind them. "What was that?"

Chapter Six

"We'll get into trouble," someone whispered.

"Don't be a baby. All the teachers are asleep. Don't you want to see what's inside this? Are you scared?"

"No!" But the voice did sound scared, the kittens thought.

"Who are they?" Tasha breathed. "Burglars?"

Peter stifled a snort. "No! It must be some of those children from the sleepover. Didn't you hear them talking about teachers?"

"But they aren't supposed to be in here!" Tasha peered round a display case, trying to see the intruders.

"Well, neither are we," Peter pointed out. "They must have crept out of the Dinosaur Gallery."

"Oh!" Tasha turned to look at Boris and Peter, her eyes suddenly wide. "Of course! That's where Bianca must be. In the Dinosaur Gallery. She loved the children; she spent all day following them around. Why didn't we think of that before?"

"Yes, why didn't we?" Boris grumbled. "I could have been fast asleep for hours.

Right, now we've got that sorted, can we go back to the cellars? I'm exhausted."

"No!" Peter and Tasha both said at once.

"We still need to find Bianca," Tasha went on.

"And we can't just leave those two," Peter added. "I don't trust them at all. Aren't they the ones who were trying to climb up the stegosaurus earlier on? And what did they mean about seeing what's inside? Inside what?" He padded further into the gallery and lurked behind a stone statue of a lion-headed goddess. Tasha and Boris came to join him.

The two children, a girl and a boy, were standing beside a huge stone sarcophagus that was one of the Egyptology department's prized exhibits. Most of the huge coffins were wooden and were protected by glass cases, but this one lay on a plinth, its great lid raised a little so visitors could peer inside at the hieroglyphics carved into the stone. The boy was pointing a torch down into the dark depths of the sarcophagus.

"There isn't anything in it," Tasha whispered crossly. "It says so on all the signs! The wooden coffin and the mummy that *were* inside it are over there in that case! Didn't they listen to anything when the staff showed them around?"

Boris sniffed. "I didn't know that, Tasha, and I live here. Besides, those two don't look to me as though they're very good at listening."

Tasha sighed sadly. She loved the museum and all the artefacts so much, it made her very cross when people didn't pay attention.

"I expect their tour was quite long," Peter said sympathetically. "Some of the guides do go on a bit, you know."

"Only because there's so much to tell..."

Tasha crept forwards, watching the two children. Were they seriously about to climb inside the mummy case? She really didn't think that was a very good idea. But the girl was standing up on the platform now, gripping the edge of the stone coffin and trying to scramble over the side.

"They won't fit, will they?" Peter asked anxiously. "I mean, we would, if we were silly enough to want to climb inside, but there isn't room for a child to get through that gap!"

"I don't know, they're quite skinny," Boris said, looking at the coffin with his head on one side. "I wonder what would happen if they bumped into those metal bits holding it open. Do you think the lid would come down and shut them inside?"

Peter squeaked in horror at the thought and the two children whirled round.

"What was that?"

The kittens shot back behind the lion statue.

"Ooops," Peter said.

"Was it a ghost?" the boy muttered, backing away from the coffin. "There's all these mummies in here. I don't like it, Lucy, we'd better get back to the others."

"It can't have been a ghost. Ghosts don't squeak," the girl said stubbornly.

"Are you thinking what I'm thinking?" Peter whispered to the other two.

"Yes!" Tasha's eyes were glowing with excitement.

Boris blinked at him. "I hardly ever think…"

"We need them out of here! The museum would be in a lot of trouble if two silly children got themselves stuck in a sarcophagus, wouldn't they?" Peter nudged him gleefully. "So let's be ghosts!"

"Oh. All right. What does a ghost do?" Boris asked.

"They make spooky noises. Do your howl, Boris," Tasha begged.

Smoke had always said there must be a Siamese somewhere in their family, because Boris could make the most eerie wailing sounds. He fluffed up the fur round his shoulders proudly, then let out a weird shriek that really did sound like a ghost, and not a happy one.

"Yes, and again!" Peter glanced at the two children as another ghostly noise echoed through the gallery. "You've got them worried, Boris, look at them, they're shaking! Ha, he's dropped the torch! Oh, I wish Bianca was here, we need something white floating around."

"What would you do, dangle her by her tail off a statue?" Boris grumbled, taking a break from wailing. "She got us into this."

"Well, we wouldn't be here to help the museum if we weren't looking for her," Tasha protested. "Do your howl again!"

Boris lifted up his head. "Wow-ow-ow-owl!"

"Oh, look, I think they're going to run for it!" Tasha purred delightedly.

The children raced away, white-faced and panicked, and the kittens trotted after them.

"Just one more, Boris, to chase them back to the Dinosaur Gallery!" Peter said, and Boris gave another long howl, one that made Peter and Tasha's fur stand on end.

"How do you do that? It's awful," Peter said admiringly.

The children sped up and shot back into the Dinosaur Gallery. The kittens watched as they flung themselves into their sleeping bags, burrowing inside and pulling the hoods over their heads.

"Did you hear that?" someone murmured, and the kittens pressed themselves flat against the wall as two teachers hurried across the room, holding torches. "Was it one of the children?"

"It didn't sound like a child…" the other one said, her voice shaking a little. "It was absolutely horrible."

Boris fanned out his whiskers grandly.

"Perhaps it was something to do with the water pipes? They did have that flood here, didn't they?"

"Oh, maybe… But it was such a ghostly sort of sound. Ugh. I suppose I'm just imagining things. Thank goodness none of the children seem to have woken up."

"You know who else hasn't woken up?" Tasha said grimly. "Bianca. And there's no way she'd have stayed asleep with Boris howling like that. Not even if she was right down inside a sleeping bag keeping someone's toes warm. She'd have known it was Boris right away and she'd have been straight over here to tell him off."

Peter nodded. "She isn't here."

"I just wish I'd said I'd go and guard that China and Glass Room." Boris heaved a massive sigh. "It's so boring in there, I might actually have got some sleep. And ever since we had that argument, it's been nothing but fuss and bother. All right. Where are we going to look for her next?"

❧ Chapter Seven ❧

Bianca was hunched up by the dolls'
house door, her ears flattened. What was
she going to do?

She had been so determined that the
other kittens wouldn't find out how
foolish she had been. Being tricked by
rats! They'd never let her live it down. But
now she didn't have a choice. She needed
someone to rescue her. Better for it to be

the kittens who let her out and not the Old Man, or one of the other museum staff.

She sat up, her whiskers drooping, and called, "Help! I'm stuck!" Somehow it was very hard to shout for help. How would anyone have heard that? It had been more of a polite whisper.

She tried again. "Tasha! Boris! Peter! Please help!"

No answer. *But then, why would there be?* Bianca thought miserably. They were probably fast asleep down in the cellars. They wouldn't be looking for her, not when she had been so sulky and mean all day…

Bianca let out a tiny mew of shame and rubbed one white paw over her

ears. Grooming always made her
feel better. Except that this time she
bumped her paw into a perfect replica
of a grandfather clock, which let out a
tinny little chime. She stared around
her. Suddenly the dolls' furniture started
making her feel that she was far too
big. Almost as if she was a giant. Could
the house really be shrinking? Bianca
shuddered. That was silly – she was
letting being
shut in get to
her.

   But when she
called again,
there was a shrill,
panicked edge to
her cries.

Still no answer. Bianca hissed and spat and swiped her claws viciously at a tiny umbrella stand filled with umbrellas about the size of her paw. Then she whirled round and shot into the drawing room. She had seen a fireplace in there, with a painted fire flickering over its coals – but there was a real opening above the fire as if the house actually had a chimney. There was a dusty-faced chimney-sweep doll standing in the kitchen, drinking a cup of tea with the cook.

Frantically, Bianca squashed into the gap above the painted coals and tried to wriggle her way up the chimney.

It was very tight. And smooth too – there was hardly any way to grip against the wooden walls. But panic gave Bianca a strength she'd never known she had. She scratched and scrabbled and squeezed her way up – until she found herself stuck. Perhaps the chimney narrowed a little, or the old wood it was made from had warped and bent, she didn't know. She simply couldn't go any further and the walls seemed to be pressing in on her. Bianca sucked in a breath to mew with fright and felt the chimney grow even tighter.

"Help! Help! Help! Oh, Tasha, Ma, someone, please get me ouuuuuut!" she wailed. Then she ran out of breath entirely and dropped back down the chimney like a stone. She fell into the fireplace, knocking over the tiny poker and shovel, and lay on the hearthrug whimpering to herself.

What if one of the museum staff saw her, squashed up in here? She'd be in so much trouble.

Bianca shivered. What if the museum staff *didn't* find her?

What if she was stuck here in this horrible little house forever?

"Good, she's stopped yowling," Dusty said, poking her nose round the old rocking horse. "I was worried she'd have one of the other kittens coming after us, making all that noise."

"I thought that's what we wanted?" Morris said, wrinkling his nose. "You said we were trying to get them all into trouble." The museum cats had been very much on their tails recently, and the rats were convinced it was entirely the kittens' fault.

Dusty nodded. "Oh, we are! One down, three to go! We're going to wreak a dreadful revenge!"

The other rats looked at her admiringly. Dusty was very good with words.

"When I've worked out how to do it," Dusty added. "Anyway, we don't want the kittens coming up here now and letting her out, do we?"

"Definitely not," Luther growled. "Fluffy little horror. Do her good to be shut up on her own for a while."

Pip gripped his tail in his paws and giggled. "Just think of her stuck in there with all that silly plaster food!"

All four rats sniggered gleefully and then they slunk out of the gallery to look for something real to eat.

All alone in the dolls' house, Bianca crawled over to the green velvet sofa and lay down, shivering sadly. At last, she wriggled herself into a white furry ball and fell into a restless sleep. She dreamed strange, frightening dreams where she was still stuck in the chimney, and the painted fire grew hotter and hotter, singing the end of her tail.

When she woke at last it seemed darker than ever. Even with her perfect cat sight, Bianca could hardly make out the shapes of the dolls' house furniture. It had to be the middle of the night, she thought. She sat on the velvet sofa and mewed quietly to herself, wishing she hadn't been so stubborn and nasty to the others.

No one had come looking for her. No one cared.

Perhaps she should leave the museum after all? If she ever got out of this terrible place...

She had given up on the idea of leaving when she had been so furious with the rats. All the pride and history of the museum cats had risen up inside her and sent her chasing after them – but it had been a mistake! The rats had been too clever for her and she had ended up trapped, and now no one could be bothered to rescue her, not her mother, or her brother and sister, or Peter!

Bianca pressed her nose into the hard little cushions and wailed.

❧ Chapter Eight ❧

Tasha, Boris and Peter had spent the
whole night going in and out of the
various rooms, calling for Bianca. They
had run into several museum cats on
their guard rounds, but everyone knew
that Boris and Bianca had had a fight.
The older cats seemed to think it was
a silly argument. No one else seemed
worried about Bianca.

Eventually, so late that it was almost early, the three kittens had slumped down on the padded seat of an old tram in the Transport Galleries. They were too tired to make it back to the cellars.

"Just a short nap," Boris yawned, and Tasha nodded. Peter was so exhausted that he fumbled the jump up to the seat and Boris had to grab him by the scruff of his neck and haul him up.

"We'll have a little sleep and then go back to searching," Tasha said drowsily. "We'll wake each other up, won't we?"

Peter tucked his tail over his nose – the Transport Galleries were a big open space and it was draughty. "Of course…"

Tasha woke a while later to heavy footsteps echoing through the room. She sprang up, her fur rising and her whiskers tense. It was completely light – they had slept through until morning.

"Wake up!" she hissed to the others. "Wake up, quick! We need to get out of here – the museum staff are coming."

"Did we oversleep?" Peter popped up his head to look out of the window.

"Come on, Boris!" Tasha leaned down and pulled Boris's whiskers hard with her teeth. "Wake up! There'll be visitors in here any minute."

Boris rolled off the seat and hit the floor with a *floof*. Then he sat up indignantly and glared at the other two. "Did you push me?"

"No!" Tasha sighed. "Be quiet, Boris.
We have to sneak out – it's morning.
And we still don't know where Bianca is.
Come on."

The three kittens peered carefully
round the back platform of the tram,
checking for museum staff, but luckily
none of them were near. Then they
hopped down and sped across the huge
hangar that housed the transport exhibits,
darting in and out of buses and trains and
shooting under the submarine.

The museum was still quiet, with only a few staff bustling about. "It must be just before opening time," Tasha whispered as they padded round the edge of the Great Hall.

"What's that noise?" Boris said, his ears twitching. "Something's going on. In the café?"

It turned out to be the children from the sleepover eating breakfast – or, in some cases, flicking yogurt at each other across the tables. Tasha looked around hopefully but Bianca wasn't with them.

"I bet she's back downstairs in the cellars, fast asleep," Boris said with a huge yawn. The chilly Transport Galleries had left him stiff and grumpy.

"We'd better put in an appearance

at breakfast anyway," Peter added. "Otherwise your ma's going to wonder what we've been doing."

They scurried down to the cellars but Bianca was nowhere to be seen. Tasha hardly ate anything, so Boris had almost all of her breakfast instead of the half she'd promised. But he didn't insist on licking out the dishes like he usually did.

"What are we going to do?" Tasha whispered. "I think we should talk to

Ma again. Or Grandpa Ivan. We need to make them see that Bianca really has disappeared. Everyone thinks she's gone off in a huff, but I'm sure it's not just that." She swallowed hard. "What if she's left the museum?" she said, glancing worriedly between the other two.

Peter wrinkled his muzzle. "What, you mean she's wandered off and got lost?"

"No… I mean actually left. Because she doesn't want to be a museum cat any more. She likes being petted and played with and admired. Maybe she's decided to go and find a different home. Maybe she wants an owner."

Peter and Boris looked doubtful. "She wouldn't," Boris said firmly. "We don't do that."

"She was so cross, though." Tasha sighed. "And she loved those children."

Boris's tail twitched. "Mmmm. Well. We could go and check the café again. Bianca wouldn't want to risk getting covered in yogurt. Perhaps she was staying out of the way."

But the café was empty when the kittens got back upstairs and the children were marching through the Grand Hall in a long line, laden with backpacks and sleeping bags.

"They must be going back to their coach," Tasha said, looking for the girl with the blond plaits who had been making such a fuss of Bianca.

"Are you looking for the little fluffy white one?" someone asked, and Tasha swung round in horrified amazement.

A rat was talking to her!

It was a smallish, pale grey rat, with very bright eyes, and it was peering round the foot of a statue up above them.

"A rat!" Boris growled, and he drew himself back, ready to spring up on to the statue's plinth.

"Wait!" Tasha squeaked, jumping in front of him. "Didn't you hear? She's talking about Bianca."

"You can understand what it said?" Boris asked, staring at her.

"Yes, of course I can! She just speaks a bit differently, that's all." Tasha gazed up at the rat. "Have you seen our sister?"

"Don't talk to it!" Boris hissed. "That's our mortal enemy, Tasha. You can't sit down with it for a chat!"

The rat gave a ratty little snigger.

"Shut up, you!" Boris snapped.

"Don't you want to hear what I've got to say?" the rat asked him in a sing-song sort of voice.

"Tasha, I think Boris is right, I don't think we should be talking to it," Peter whispered. "I don't trust it."

"Shh!" Tasha put her front paws up against the plinth. "Please! Don't listen to them. I want to know. Have you seen Bianca? We've lost her."

"It's the rats," Boris said. "I bet it is! Why didn't we think of it before? They've taken her. Rouse the guards! Call out the cats! The rats have kitnapped Bianca!"

Tasha whirled round and growled loudly in Boris's face. "Be quiet! Even if they have, which I don't believe anyway, how are we ever going to know where she is if you don't let this rat tell us?"

Boris stepped back, muttering furiously, and the grey rat peered down at Tasha. "Thank you! You're clearly the brains of the operation."

"Just get on with it," Peter snarled at the grey rat.

"I'm trying!" The rat leaned a little closer to Tasha. "Brothers … I know how you feel. But anyway … your sister's on the coach."

Tasha gasped. "I was right! She's leaving the museum!"

"Mm-hm. She's gone off with those children. Thought you might like to know. Ta-ta!" The rat shot away, round the back of the stone figure, and Boris leaped after it. But the tiny passage the rat disappeared into was too small for a cat and all he did was crumple his whiskers.

"Gone. Nasty little sneak."

"Never mind. We need to get after Bianca! We have to get her back!" Tasha looked around wildly, wondering which was the quickest way to the side of the museum where the coaches were parked.

"I'm not sure I believe that rat," Peter said slowly.

Boris's whiskers twitched. "Exactly! Why would they suddenly decide to do us a favour? We spend all our time chasing them!"

"I don't know," Tasha admitted. "But we have to make sure. What if the rat was telling the truth and we let Bianca go off without trying to stop her?" She raced out on to the terrace, galloping as fast as she could, and the other two hurried after her.

"Tasha!" Peter panted. "If Bianca wants to run away, what are we going to do about it?"

"We have to tell her we love her!" Tasha called back over her shoulder. "I'm not letting her go without telling her that!"

🐾 Chapter Nine 🐾

The three kittens rushed round the
outside of the building to the coach park,
which wasn't far from the river. Luckily,
there was only one coach parked there
so early and they could see the last few
children from the sleepover climbing on.

"Tasha, they'll see us," Peter hissed.
"You can't just get on the coach. What
about all those teachers?"

"I don't care!" Tasha called back. "And I expect the teachers will be too busy counting children to notice."

Peter and Boris exchanged anxious glances, but they followed Tasha up the steps. One of the children was carrying a large backpack in her hand, and they were able to sneak along beside it and then dart under the first row of seats. The coach was much more modern than the old buses in the Transport Galleries.

It was also very noisy. All the children seemed to be talking at once, and Tasha turned worried eyes on Peter and Boris. "I was going to call for Bianca, but I don't think she'll hear me over all this shouting."

"We'll have to hunt for her," Boris said,

peering out at the feet of the children in the next row. "We'd smell her if she was hiding in one of their bags, wouldn't we?"

"I think so," Tasha agreed. She looked daunted for a moment. "So we have to sniff every bag?"

"How else are we going to do it?" Boris said grimly. "Come on."

It was all very well saying it, but sniffing every child's bag for a hidden kitten wasn't that easy. Lots of the children had their bags on their laps, showing each other the things they had bought in the museum shop, or searching for that last packet of sweets. The kittens had to keep reaching up to get a sniff of the bags and it was very hard not to be noticed. Tasha was just peeping up round the side of a seat to inspect a bright pink backpack, when one of the teachers leaned over.

"Bella, what's that?" She was pointing directly at Tasha.

Tasha froze for a second and then dropped down on to the floor, paws limp. She stared fixedly ahead, trying to look as much like a toy kitten as she could.

"Oh, it's just
your toy cat. Put
it in your bag, Bella.
You don't want to leave it
behind on the coach, do you?" The teacher
passed on up the gangway and the two
girls stared at Tasha, their mouths open.

"You didn't bring a toy cat, did you?"
the girl sitting next to Bella whispered.

"No... It's one of the kittens from the
museum!" Bella whispered back, her
eyes fixed on the slumped tabby kitten. "I
remember her! I saw her when we were
in the gardens. There were lots of cats out
there, Millie, don't you remember? What's
she doing? Do you think she's all right?"

"She was pretending to be a toy for
Miss Williams," Millie said slowly. "That

119

was really clever."

Tasha sat up, dabbed her nose gratefully against Bella's hand and then rubbed her head on Millie's cardigan. Then she slipped back under the seats again.

The two girls leaned out into the aisle to watch her. "What's she up to?" Millie said. "What's she doing on our coach?"

Bella shook her head. "I don't know. But whatever it is, we're not going to stop her!"

At the back of the coach, Tasha found Boris and Peter, who both looked frazzled.

"One of the boys tried to put *me* in his backpack!" Peter complained. "I nearly had to scratch him."

"We'd better hurry up and find Bianca," Boris growled. "Or the teachers are going to realize something's going on.

The children are all whispering about us. I don't think we were as sneaky as we meant to be."

"I didn't catch so much as a sniff of her, though," Tasha said. "I think you two were right. I'm sorry. That rat was playing a trick on us."

"I don't want to say I told you so…" Boris began. But then he stopped and fanned out his whiskers. "Actually, yes, I do. I told you so."

Tasha brightened up. "I suppose it's good news. Bianca didn't want to run away from the museum after all!"

"Yes, and we don't have to persuade her to change her mind," Boris pointed out. "Which is good, because she's very stubborn."

Tasha and Peter exchanged glances, and then the fur rose up all along Tasha's back.

"What is it?"

"The engine! Can't you feel it? The coach driver's turned the engine on!" Tasha popped her head out and peered down the aisle. "We're leaving!"

The three kittens stared at each other in horror. Then, as one, they streaked down the coach towards the closing door.

Squeaks and yelps and wild giggling followed them, and one of the teachers reached out to try and grab Peter as he shot past. He gave a panicked mew and jinked sideways to escape.

"Come on! It's nearly shut!" Tasha cried as she dived out of the door after Boris.

Peter took a flying leap from the top of the steps and squeezed through the door just as it thumped shut. The coach shuddered and growled away, with the three kittens staring after it.

"My tail!" Peter mewed. "I can't look! How much of it have I got left?"

"It's fine," Tasha purred soothingly. "It's a teensy little bit bald at the very tip, that's all. If I didn't know you'd nearly had it shut in a door, I'd never have noticed." She barged Boris hard in the side. "You wouldn't either, would you?"

"Well … oh, I mean, no. Definitely not."

Boris and Tasha sat down on either side of Peter, and the little black kitten closed his eyes and slumped wearily in the sun. "Now what are we going to do?" he said. "She wasn't on the coach. She isn't anywhere in the museum. She's just … disappeared."

"I still think it's something to do with the rats," Tasha said, flexing her claws in and out in a thoughtful sort of way. "Oh, I know they were lying about Bianca being on the coach. But what if they've got something to do with her going missing? That grey rat knew something, I'm sure she did."

Boris snorted. "Yeah, it knew you were a soft touch."

"But we've looked everywhere, Boris!" Tasha pointed out. "You said before that the rats had kitnapped her. I think maybe you were right."

Boris stared at her in surprise. "Oh! Really?"

"Yes." Tasha showed her teeth in a decisive snarl. "So now we have to make them give her back!"

Chapter Ten

"How are we going to track down those rats?" Peter swallowed hard. "Boris was too big to get into that hole behind the statue, but maybe I could fit."

"No!" Boris said fiercely, and Peter jumped back in fright. His poor tail was still making him feel wobbly.

"Sorry. I mean, you mustn't do that." Boris gave Peter's ears an encouraging lick. "We don't know how many rats are in those tunnels – there could be hundreds of them. If I'd been thinking straight, I'd never have tried to get down there either. It was just seeing that rat shoot into the hole – my ratting instinct took over." Then he sat up straighter, looking shocked. "I've had an idea!"

Tasha snorted. "Don't hurt yourself."

"Very funny." Boris stared down his own whiskers, going almost cross-eyed. "Yes. Actually, I think it's a good idea. We should go and hang around the back of the museum café, by the bins. It's the rats' favourite place – they sneak about there all the time. Then when they've finished scavenging, we follow them. If they've really kitnapped Bianca, they'll have to go and check on her sometime, won't they?"

"Sounds like a good idea to me," Peter said, trying not to sound surprised.

Boris sat up proudly. "I knew hanging around the bins would be useful one day. Come on!"

The kittens crept round the back of the building to the little yard behind the café and Boris gave the huge metal bins a professional once-over. "Not the best time – they haven't put out the lunch leftovers yet. But you never know." They ducked behind a bicycle that had been left leaning against the wall and fixed their eyes on the bins.

"Look, there…" Peter breathed, nudging the other two. "I'm sure I saw a tail under that bin!"

The three kittens watched as dark shadows scurried under the bins and a line of rats passed scraps down the side. It was hard to watch without feeling hungry and Boris was actually drooling.

"They're going!" Tasha hissed at last. "Get ready to sneak after them. Not too close."

The rats slunk away through a gap in the wall and the kittens followed.

"Where on earth are they going?" Boris muttered as the rats went up and down and round the museum.

"We ought to try and remember all these holes and cut-throughs," Peter said. "I bet even Grandpa Ivan doesn't know about that swinging door under the stuffed wolf."

"Shh, they'll hear us." Tasha stopped suddenly. "I think we're going to come out in the Dolls' Houses and Toys Gallery. What can they be doing there?"

The four rats peeped out cautiously from behind a rocking horse, checking that there were no visitors nearby.

Then they pattered across the gallery in a line past the Meccano and underneath the enormous clockwork train layout. They gathered in a horseshoe round one of the dolls' houses – a huge one with a blue roof and a long veranda along the first floor.

Tasha, Peter and Boris sneaked out behind them.

"Can you hear anything?" one of the rats asked. Tasha was almost sure it was the grey rat that had told them Bianca was on the coach.

"Not a thing." The largest rat, a big brown one with a fat, snaky tail, sounded quite cheerful about that. "She's probably keeled over under that little kitchen table in a dead faint. That'll teach her. And we've sent the others off on a coach to who knows where! Excellent work, my friends."

"What did you do to her?" Boris yowled, leaping forwards. "That's my sister you're talking about, you monstrous mouse!"

"Oi, not so much of the mouse!" the rat snapped back, whipping round and baring his long yellow teeth at Boris. "There's four of us and only three of you, matey."

"And Luther's bigger than you are!" piped up the littlest rat, who was only a smidge smaller than Peter was. The museum did seem to breed large rats…

"He's right," Tasha whispered. "Oh, be careful, Boris!"

Boris was fluffing up every hair,
making himself look as big as he possibly
could. His tail was at least three times
its usual size. But the rats were gathered
in a knot round the huge Luther now,
cheering him on as he stepped forwards,
his own tail snapping and coiling.

Boris was about to spring on them, with Tasha and Peter close behind, when all four rats suddenly pulled up short. The chief rat, Luther, looked up, and then up some more, and then he whisked round and made a flying leap for the dolls' house plinth. The other three rats scampered after him and the kittens turned round.

Smoke was standing behind them, looking very large indeed.

"I'm quite sure you would have sent those rats packing," she told Boris, nudging his nose affectionately with hers. "But I thought you might just need a little help."

"Have you been following us?" Tasha asked suspiciously.

"Only since you went to stake out the bins. Which was a very clever idea," Smoke added with a glance at Boris, who brightened up a bit. "I was worried about your sister. I'm sorry, kittens. I should have listened to you last night, but I thought Bianca needed some time to come to her senses."

Peter's ears twitched and he turned back to stare at the dolls' house. "I can hear something," he said. Then he let out a yelp. "Look! Look up at the house!"

There at the drawing-room window, framed in the lace curtains, was Bianca. Her blue eyes were wide and frantic, and she was bouncing up and down, banging on the glass with her paws.

"Get me out! Please get me out!" she mewed, her voice thin and squeaky with fright.

Boris leaped for the dolls' house, knocking out the hook that held the hinged front in place. It swung open slowly and Bianca scrambled out, scrabbling her way down the plinth to land at her mother's feet in a puddle of scruffy white fur.

"I thought no one was coming!" she wailed.

"We were out looking for you all night!" Tasha said, nosing her lovingly. "We got stuck on a coach and Peter nearly lost his tail, just for you!"

"You did what?" Smoke muttered, her ears flat against her head. "Oh, glory…"

"And Boris was about to fight the biggest rat you've ever seen," Peter said. "He had teeth like tombstones, Bianca!"

Bianca looked up. "They shut me in. I was chasing them because they were frightening the children at the sleepover. Some of them were crying!"

"That certainly shouldn't be allowed to happen!" Smoke gave Bianca an approving nod.

"You chased those rats all on your own?" Boris said, impressed.

Bianca sighed. "I didn't know it was all of them. I thought it was just one rat, although I did wonder why it kept changing colour. They were extremely sneaky – they kept pretending to be each other…"

"Hush," Smoke murmured. "I hear visitors. Back to the cellars, kittens." She reached up and pushed the front of the dolls' house closed with one paw. "You've had enough adventuring for a while, I think. And it sounds to me as if you all need a proper sleep. Especially if you're going to be on guard duty together tonight…"

"Bianca. Bianca, wake up…" Boris licked her nose gently. "It's supper time. We go on watch soon. And I brought you a present."

Bianca yawned and blinked at him.

It felt so good, sleeping on the tattered tapestries, with Tasha curled up on one side and Peter on the other. It was exactly where she belonged.

"Where have you been?" Tasha demanded, looking up at Boris.

"Out," Boris said loftily. "Bianca, look." He pushed something towards her with his nose and Bianca's whiskers twitched as she saw it sparkle.

Boris looked proud. "I made it. It's a...
Oh, I can't remember the name of it. A
sparkly thing – for you."

"A tiara." Bianca sniffed thoughtfully at
the silvery ring. "It smells of fish!"

"Tuna." Boris nodded. "It was the foil
from the Old Man's sandwiches. I rescued
it out of a bin. Do you like it?" he asked
hopefully. "There's green bits too, like on
that one in the Jewel Room. They're only
chocolate wrappers, though..."

Bianca touched noses with him, and
Boris picked up the tiara in his teeth
and dropped it on top of her head, a bit
lopsided. "There!"

"It's ever so grand, Bianca," Peter said
admiringly. "You look like one of those

old portraits in the galleries upstairs.
Very proper for a museum kitten."

"Do you like it?" Boris asked, giving his
sister a hopeful look.

Bianca sat up straight, curled her tail
perfectly round her paws and closed her
eyes. "I love it!"

Author's Note

I really enjoyed writing this Museum
Kittens adventure. One of the best bits
of this series for me is thinking about
all the museum exhibits that the kittens
come across in their adventures.
Tasha is me, with her love of the stories
behind the artefacts!

The Dolls' Houses and Toys Gallery is
loosely based on the V&A Museum of
Childhood at Bethnal Green in London, but
the dolls' house that the rats trap Bianca in
is mine! My mother had a beautiful dolls'
house when I was growing up, which I was
allowed to keep in my bedroom.

There was something about the tiny people and their delicate furniture that I loved, and I still do. So much so that I now have a dolls' house of my own, with a hinged front, a long balcony, and a kitchen full of copper jelly moulds and quite a lot of plaster food...

From MULTI-MILLION best-selling author

Holly Webb

Museum
Kittens

The Midnight Visitor

Illustrated by Sarah Lodge

One stormy night
a little black kitten is left
on the museum steps.

Tasha is eager to show Peter
the hidden passages and secret
corners, though not all the
kittens are so welcoming.

The pair set out to catch the
rat that's been stealing from the
Dinosaur Gallery. But when they
have a spine-chilling run-in with
a tyrannosaurus, will anyone
come to their rescue?

Read on for an extract from Book 1

The Midnight Visitor

"Mrrrowww." Tasha rolled over and waved her tiny striped paws in the air. The wide stone steps that led up to the museum entrance were warm from the sun and she was so deliciously sleepy. There was a light breeze blowing off the river and she could hear gulls calling over the water.

"You're getting your fur dirty, Tasha," said a disapproving voice, and the tabby kitten opened one green eye to see who was talking to her. "Ma says we mustn't get our fur dirty – we should be clean and neat at all times."

"Oh hush, Bianca." Tasha closed her eye again, but it was no good. Her sister was still there – she could feel her. Bianca was blocking out the spring sunshine and now the afternoon felt dull and chilly.

"Ma says," Bianca insisted. She sat down next to Tasha and started to wash. She didn't need to – her white fur was spotless as always. Even her paw pads were perfectly pink and it looked as though she'd combed her beautiful whiskers.

Tasha rolled over and sprang up, peering over her shoulder at her grey and black tabby stripes. Bianca was right. She was covered in dust and her fur was sticking up all over the place. Half her whiskers seemed to be stuck together too – she wasn't sure how that had happened. She had gone exploring through the museum workshop earlier on. Perhaps she shouldn't have looked so closely at that pot of varnish. She stuck out her tongue to try and reach her sticky whiskers, but it didn't work.

"You are a disgrace to the museum," Bianca said, stopping mid wash with one paw in the air. "Just look at the state of you. Tch."

"I'm not!" Tasha said crossly. "We're supposed to be here to keep the mice and rats away. The rats don't care if my whiskers are tangled. It doesn't matter if I'm clean or not."

"Ma won't agree," Bianca purred, twitching her whiskers at a pair of visitors walking past them up the steps. "See? They thought I was adorable. They just said so. They didn't even notice you."

Tasha considered leaping on her sister's

head and rolling her over in the dust. Then she wouldn't be so perfect. But Tasha would only get into trouble. Ma might keep her downstairs in the cellars in the museum cats' den until bedtime, instead of letting her explore the museum and the courtyard and the gardens with the others.

"Come here," Bianca sighed, leaning over to lick the scruffy fur on Tasha's back. "I'll tidy you up."

Tasha's whiskers bristled as Bianca licked her fur straight. She sat hunched over with her ears flat back, letting out little outraged hisses.

"Don't make such a fuss! If you don't like being washed, you shouldn't get yourself in such a mess."

From MULTI-MILLION best-selling author

Holly Webb

Museum Kittens

The Pharaoh's Curse

Illustrated by Sarah Lodge

The kittens are curious when
a rare Egyptian treasure is brought
to the museum.

From the moment the object arrives,
rumours of an ancient curse begin
to spread. But Tasha is determined
to prove to the other kittens that
there's nothing to be afraid of.

Then a pipe bursts and the
gallery is flooded – the kittens are
trapped! Are they the latest victims
of the pharaoh's curse?

HOLLY WEBB

Holly Webb started out as a children's book editor and wrote her first series for the publisher she worked for. She has been writing ever since, with over one hundred books to her name. Holly lives in Berkshire, with her husband and three children. Holly's pet cats are always nosying around when she is trying to type on her laptop.

For more information about Holly Webb visit:

www.holly-webb.com